Rosie & Jim
and the Man in the Wind

Written by John Cunliffe

Illustrated by Celia Berridge

Based on the Central Independent Television Series produced by Ragdoll Productions

Hippo Books
Scholastic Children's Books
London

Scholastic Children's Books,
Scholastic Publications Ltd,
7-9 Pratt Street, London NW1 0AE, UK

Scholastic Inc.,
730 Broadway, New York, NY 10003, USA

Scholastic Canada Ltd,
123 Newkirk Road, Richmond Hill,
Ontario, Canada L4C 3G5

Ashton Scholastic Pty Ltd,
P O Box 579, Gosford, New South Wales,
Australia

Ashton Scholastic Ltd,
Private Bag 1, Penrose, Auckland,
New Zealand

First published in hardback by Scholastic Publications Ltd, 1992
This edition published, 1992

Based on the Central Television series
Produced by Ragdoll Productions

ISBN 0 590 55020 9

Typeset in Great Britain by Kalligraphic Design Ltd, Horley, Surrey
Printed by Mateu Cromo Ltd, Madrid

10 9 8 7 6 5 4 3 2 1

Rosie and Jim are on their boat, the good boat Ragdoll.
John steers the boat. Rosie and Jim look out to see what they can see.
What will they find today for John to put in his book?

The boat slowed down, and nosed its way into the river bank.
"We're stopping!" said Rosie.
John jumped ashore and tied the boat up.
"Oooh, goody," said Jim. "I wonder where we're going?"
Some little ducks swam up to the boat.
"Ooh, look," said Rosie, "they're hungry."
"Give them a bit of fizz-gog's bread," said Jim.
"Just a little bit, then," said Rosie.

When Jim looked in the bread-bin, all the bread was gone!
"Ooh, noggin," said Rosie, "we've used it all up."
"I hope John isn't hungry," said Jim.
"We'll have to get some more from the shop," said Rosie.
"There are no shops here," said Jim. "We're in the countryside."
"What fizz-pots!" said Rosie.

But John *was* feeling hungry. He went into his kitchen to make a cheese sandwich. When he looked in his bread-bin, there was no bread at all. Not so much as a crust!

"I wonder where all the bread goes to on my boat?" said John. "I'm sure I had some left this morning. And there are no shops here. Now if I had some flour, I could make some bread."

Then John looked in his waterways book, and saw something that made him smile.
"There's a windmill not far from here," he said. "I'd like to see that. And. . . if they sell flour, perhaps I can buy some and make bread with it. And I might be able to put it into a story, as well . . ."

"What's he on about?" said Rosie to Jim.
"He says he can *make* bread, if he goes to a windmill," said Jim.
"What a noggin!" said Rosie. "We'd better follow and see what he gets up to."

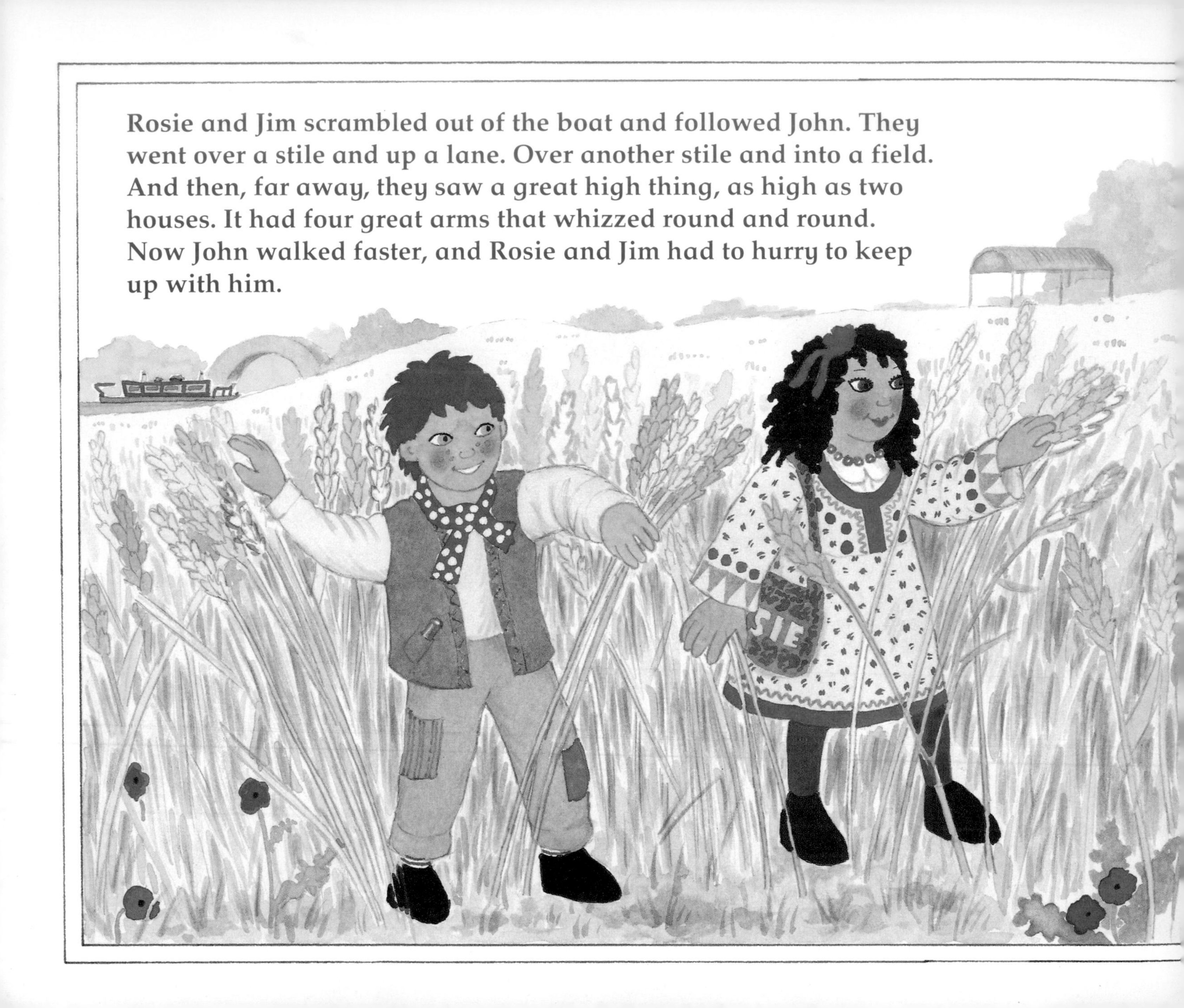

Rosie and Jim scrambled out of the boat and followed John. They went over a stile and up a lane. Over another stile and into a field. And then, far away, they saw a great high thing, as high as two houses. It had four great arms that whizzed round and round. Now John walked faster, and Rosie and Jim had to hurry to keep up with him.

They came to a field of wheat. It grew much higher than Rosie and Jim's heads, like a forest. John stopped to feel the wheat. He pulled a piece from its stalk, and rubbed it until the grains lay in his hand.

"Isn't it amazing," said John, "that this can be made into flour, and then into bread."

"He's talking to himself," said Rosie.

"And what is he on about?" said Jim. "He says you can make that stuff into bread."

"Doesn't look a bit like bread to me," said Rosie. "What a gobbin!"

Now they were near to the windmill. Rosie and Jim had never seen anything like it.
"What is it, Jim?" said Rosie. "A *wind* mill? Is it a place where they make wind?"
"I don't know," said Jim. "It's a funny whizzy place."
"It makes me dizzy," said Rosie.
"It's a whizzy house," said Jim. "And windy as well. It makes me all fozzly."
"I know," said Rosie. "The wind blows and makes it go round. That's what it does."
"But how does that make bread?" said Jim.
"Let's follow fizz-pot and see if we can find out," said Rosie.
"Look!" said Jim. "There's a man in it!"

And surely enough, there was a man, waving to John from his door high up in the side of the windmill.
"The man in the wind; like the man in the moon," said Rosie.

The sails stopped, and the man shouted to John that it was safe to come up now. John began climbing up the great ladder, up to the door of the windmill. Rosie and Jim followed.
"We're going in," said Rosie. "Ooops, up we go. Mind how you go, Jim."

And when they were all inside, the man in the wind started the mill going again. And what a rumbly-bumbly place it was! It was full of huge wooden wheels that went rumbling round, and the whole mill trembled and shook, and ground and grumbled.

There were more ladders inside, and they went up and up, to the very top of the mill. The wind blew and sighed in the sails outside, and they turned the big wheels inside. The big wooden wheels turned big stone wheels. The man in the wind had a big sack full of grains of wheat, like the ones John had looked at in the field. Rosie and Jim hid behind more sacks, and watched everything.

"What is it for?" said Jim.
"It's for making bread, Jimmy-gobbin," said Rosie.
They saw the man in the wind pour the grains from the sack into a wooden chute. The grains trickled and poured down to the floor below, until they went between two big stone wheels that ground them up into powdery stuff.

"So that's how you make the flour?" said John to the man in the wind.
"Yes," said the miller.
"And can I buy some, to make bread?" said John.
"Of course you can," said the miller.

"Did you hear that?" said Rosie to Jim. "That's flour."
"Yes," said Jim, "and you can make bread with it."

"Well, I never," said Rosie. "I never did!"

John walked home with two bags of flour from the mill, with Rosie and Jim following after him.

When they were back at the boat, Rosie and Jim watched John mixing his flour with water and sugar, a little salt and some yeast. Then he pressed it hard with his hands. He squashed it and squeezed it, and turned it over, and squashed it and squeezed it again. It was like a big piece of plasticine. He put it by the stove in a bowl, with a wet cloth over it, and went off to get some honey.

ROSIE
100%
FLOUR
100%

Rosie and Jim went to have a look at John's bread.
"Is this it?" said Rosie.
"It's all squashy," said Jim.
"If that's what he calls bread," said Rosie, "he can keep it. I'll have a sliced white from the shop."
"What a funny pong!" said Jim.
"He'll never eat that!" said Rosie.
"Come on, Rosie," said Jim, "let's play with it. It's like plasticine."

Rosie made a bread-duck.
Jim made a bread-John.
They left them by the stove, and went to look at John's book.
Then Rosie said, "Let's go and see if that squishy stuff's turned into bread, yet."
What a fright they had when they went to look.
"It's got bigger!" said Jim.

"Ooh, err," said Rosie. "It must be alive."
"And it's got a fizzy smell," said Jim.
"He's done it all wrong," said Rosie. "What a noggin. He'll have to get some shop bread, now."

Then they heard Duck quacking to warn them that John was coming back. Rosie sang their song . . .

Ducky's quacking
His quacky song!
Come on Jim
We've played too long!

. . . and they whizzed round and tidied everything up, and sat on their seat and kept as still as still, so that John would never know that they came to life. But they watched all that John did.

He put all the squashy-stuff into the hot oven. He never noticed the bread-Duck and the bread-John, but he put them in the oven, too. Then he set his table for tea. At last it was time for him to take the bread out of the oven.

What a surprise for Rosie and Jim. It had turned from that funny squishy stuff into lovely crusty brown bread. And what a surprise for John, when he found that he had a bread-Duck and a bread-John amongst his rolls and loaves of bread.

John had a lovely tea, with his fresh bread and his pot of honey. And when he went outside to start the boat again, Rosie and Jim had a feast as well. Rosie ate the bread-Duck. Jim ate the bread-John. John never knew where they had gone to. Perhaps he had only dreamed that they were there?

Soon it was time for John to tie the boat up for the night. He sat down to write his story about Rosie and Jim, and what they might have done if they could have come to life that day. This is the story he wrote . . .

One windy day Rosie and Jim saw a big whizzy thing far across the fields.

"There's a giant waving to us," said Rosie.

"Let's go and see," said Jim.

It wasn't a giant. It was a windmill, with great sails whizzing round and round. There was a man in it.

"The man in the wind," said Rosie.

The man in the wind gave
them a bag of flour.
"Mix it with water," he said,
"and make anything
you like."

They made a little house,
with chairs and tables.

The house began to grow – until it was so big that Rosie and Jim could go into the house, and sit at the table.

"Let's have a party," said Jim.

Lots of friends came. There were cows, and sheep, and hens, a horse, two ducks, a dog, and a cat.

They were all hungry.

"What shall we eat?" said Jim.

"Noggin," said Rosie. "There's nothing in the cupboard."

The cows ate the walls. The sheep ate the chairs. The cat ate the chimney.
"It's all bread, noggins," said Rosie.

Soon there was only a pile of crumbs for the little birds that flew down.
"That's the end of our magic house, fizz-pots," said Rosie.

Rosie and Jim went home to their boat. That was made of steel.
Nobody could eat *that.*